Totem Tale

Deb Vanasse Illustrations by **Erik Brooks**

PAWS IV *published by*
SASQUATCH BOOKS

Deep in a cedar forest stood a
totem pole, stark and still.
Long ago a carver stacked the totem
animals and then forgot them.

One night the moon rose low and full.
Washed in the light of moonbeams,
the totems **SPRANG** to life.

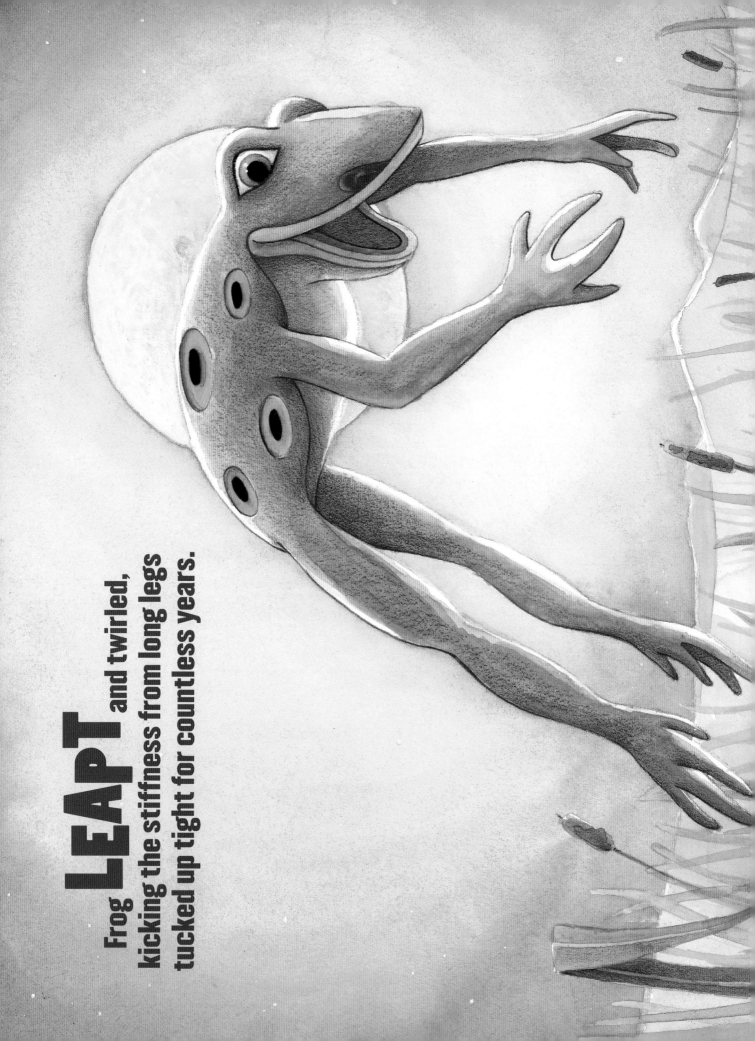

Frog **LEAPT** and twirled, kicking the stiffness from long legs tucked up tight for countless years.

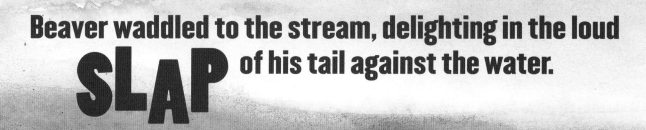

Beaver waddled to the stream, delighting in the loud **SLAP** of his tail against the water.

Eagle **SWOOPED** and dove with outstretched wings, silvery salmon darting beneath her looming shadow.

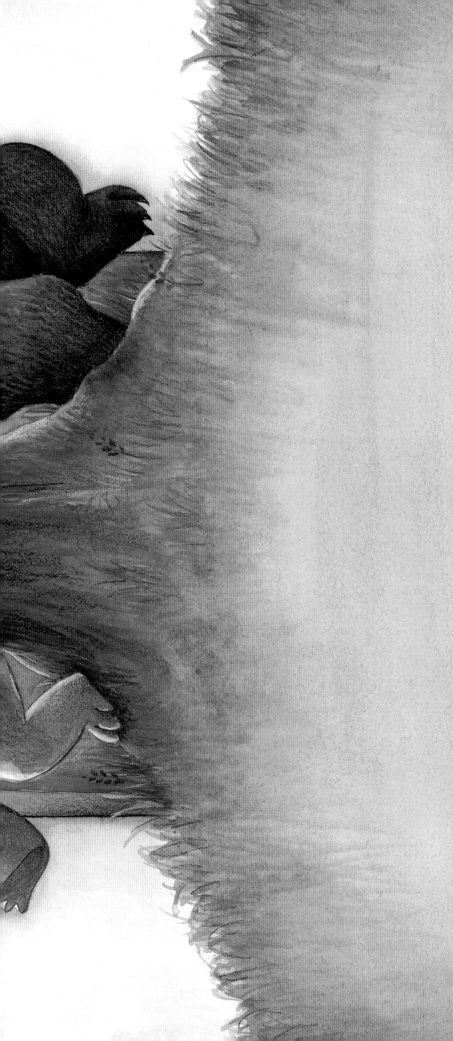

Grizzly **WRIGGLED** his back against a tall tree, growling with the relief of a long itch finally scratched.

Wolf lifted her voice toward the moon, **HOWLING** with the pure joy of silence broken.

Raven strutted, cocking his head and **CHATTERING** to himself.

All too soon, a hint of dawn brushed the blackened sky.

The totems must return to the pole, or the rising sun will trap them in the Land of In-Between and Never-There.

But none of them could remember how they fit, and each wanted the place of honor at the top of the pole.

"I'm the largest and the loudest," Grizzly roared. He shimmied to the top, but the pole **SWAYED** back and forth beneath his weight, and the totems toppled to the ground.

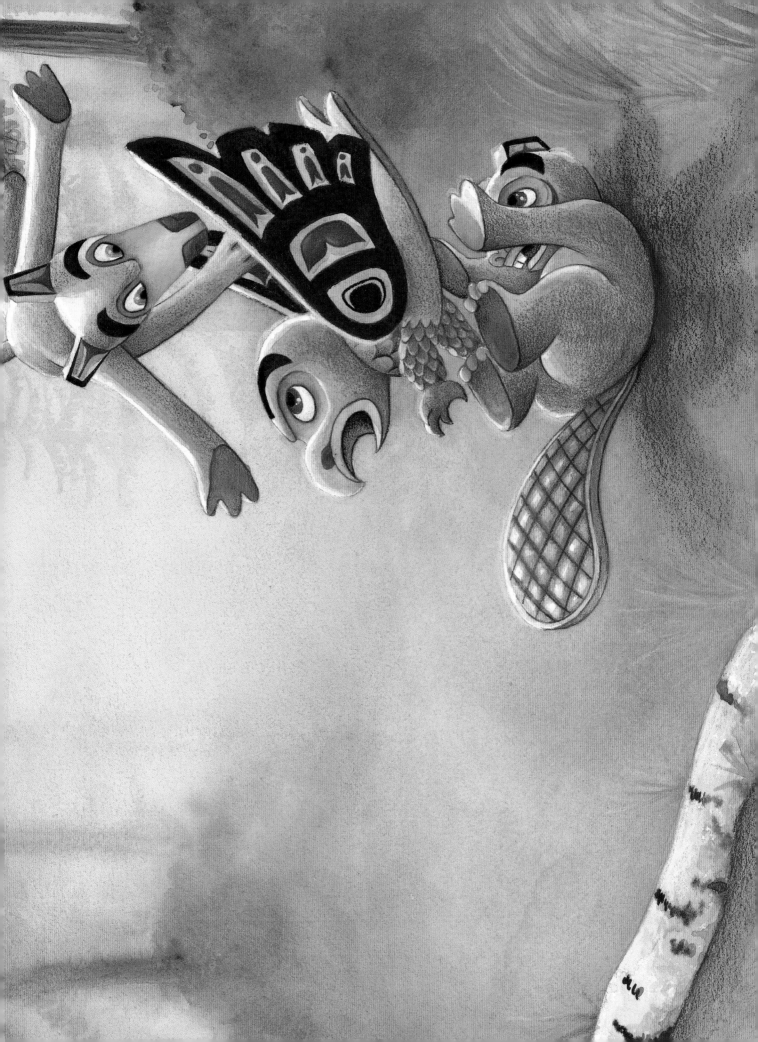

"I'm a fearless hunter," said Wolf. With a quick scamper, she took her place on top.

But her sharp claws dug into the thin skin of Eagle's neck, and down they went, one after the other.

"I have the sharpest eyes," bragged Eagle, stretching her great, wide wings to claim the highest spot.

But her tail feathers tickled Wolf's nose, and a loud **KER-CHEW** sent them tumbling again.

But he wasn't used to sitting up so high. After a

TEETERING

moment, he rolled off, taking the others with him.

"Who sings the sweetest song of night?" asked Frog.

"I don't see what singing has to do with it," grumbled Wolf, but she crouched to let the others climb up.

With a skip and a hop, Frog leapt to the very top, where she danced an excited jig that made the pole quiver and

SHAKE

till they all fell down.

"There's something you've forgotten,"
SQUAWKED
Raven, shaking his head.

"Together we told a story — a story of how Frog muddied the water to hide Beaver from danger, and how Beaver dammed the stream so Eagle could fish from a quiet pool, and how Eagle led Grizzly to a wide patch of berries, and how Grizzly shared his den with Wolf one cold winter night."

The totems looked at each other, nodding and remembering. They took their story-places — Frog, then Beaver, then Eagle, then Grizzly, then Wolf. It was a perfect fit.

Then Raven flapped and fluttered to the top as the first sunbeams shimmered over the horizon, casting the broad light of day on a story that will last forever.

To Lynx and Jess, with love.

AUTHOR'S NOTE
For more than 200 years, the indigenous cultures of the Pacific Northwest and Southeast Alaska have carved totem poles to illustrate the stories of their clans. Wrangell, Sitka, Ketchikan, Seattle, and Vancouver Island are some of the best places to see these magnificent works of art.

Text copyright ©2006 by Deb Vanasse
Illustration copyright ©2006 by Erik Brooks

Printed in China
Published by Sasquatch Books
Distributed by Publishers Group West
10 09 08   9 8 7 6 5 4 3

Book design: William Quinby

Library of Congress Cataloging-in-Publication Data is available.

ISBN 1-57061-439-3

SASQUATCH BOOKS
119 South Main Street, Suite 400 / Seattle, WA 98104 / (206) 467-4300
www.sasquatchbooks.com / custserv@sasquatchbooks.com